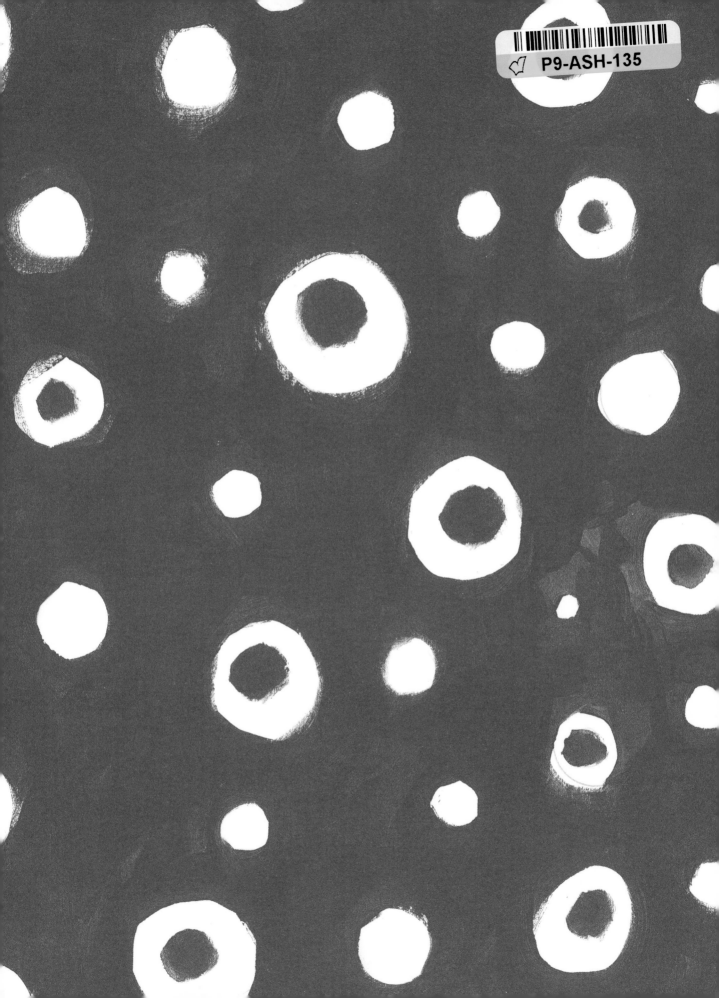

COUNTING LEOPARD'S SPOTS

To Vanessa
T.W.

For Hillary Hargraves Dix
H.O.

First Published in the United States 1998 by
Little Tiger Press
N16 W23390 Stoneridge Drive, Waukesha, WI 53188
Originally published in Great Britain 1996 by
Orchard Books, London
Text copyright © Hiawyn Oram 1996
Illustrations copyright © Tim Warnes 1996
All rights reserved.
Library of Congress Cataloging-in-Publication Data
Oram, Hiawyn
Counting Leopard's Spots and other animal stories / retold by
Hiawyn Oram ; illustrated by Tim Warnes
p.   cm.
Summary : A collection of folktales from Africa, introducing a
wide variety of animals.
ISBN 1-888444-31-2
1. Tales—Africa. [1. Folklore—Africa. 2. Animals—Folklore.]
I. Warnes, Tim, ill. II. Title
PZ7. 0624Co 1998
398. 2—dc21 97-47297 CIP AC
Printed in Dubai
First American Edition

1 3 5 7 9 10 8 6 4 2

COUNTING LEOPARD'S SPOTS

AND OTHER ANIMAL STORIES

Retold by Hiawyn Oram

Illustrated by Tim Warnes

CONTENTS PAGE

MAKE FRIENDS WITH THE ANIMALS

Zebra

Hippo

Tortoise and Osprey

Wildcat and Hyena

Leopard

YOU'LL MEET IN THE STORIES.

Lion and Hare

Tortoise and Monkey

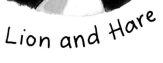

Elephant and Hippo

Bushbuck and Chameleon

Jackal and Rabbit

JUST ANOTHER MOUTHFUL

nce when the world was very new, the animals were new, too. They had no horns or fancy coats. Nothing to hide in and nothing to show off.

Of all the animals only Zebra thought this was fine.

"What do coats and horns matter?" she said. "What do appearances matter when there's so much tender new grass to eat?"

But in spite of the grass—and there was a lot of it—the other animals continued to long for coats and horns.

They continued to believe that one day they'd get them, too.

And all at once, that day came. The sun rose over the hills. The dawn mist slowly disappeared on the lake. The animals, gathering for their morning drink, lifted their heads and knew today was the day.

Somehow they knew their coats and horns were in the great cave on the other side of the plain. The animals were to go when the sun was halfway to its highest point. And it was going to be first come, first served.

With great excitement they began arranging themselves in a line to watch the sun and wait.

Only Zebra showed no interest. She was far too busy eating.

"Hey, Zebra, aren't you joining us?" called Sable the Antelope.

"Just another mouthful," said Zebra.

"But we're about to leave," called Kudu, Sable's cousin. "In fact, look at the sun. It's time."

"Just another mouthful," said Zebra as the animals sped off across the plain.

"And another . . . and another and maybe, since the grass is so new and tender . . ." she said as Elephant arrived at the cave, and Sable arrived behind Elephant, and Kudu arrived behind Sable, "another."

"And another," she said as the other animals piled up behind Kudu to stare at horns beyond their wildest dreams and coats beyond their wildest imaginings.

"And another," she said as Elephant took the best coat with an incredibly long matching nose.

"And another," she said as Sable chose a silky coat in a rich, earthy brown and a long pair of fighting horns.

"And another," she said as Kudu climbed into a gray coat with a few elegant stripes and went into ecstasies over a pair of corkscrew antlers.

"And another and another and another," she said as
the other animals delightedly made their selections
and rushed out onto the plain to prance and frisk and
hide and show off . . .

"Oh no!" said Elephant. "You're not still eating, are
you? Don't you want a coat and horns?"

"What?" said Zebra, looking up for a moment.
And now it was her turn to stare—
at the magnificence of the returning
animals in all their new finery.

"Uh, no, I'm not still eating.
I'm leaving now," she
said quickly.

And imagining herself in only the best—a nose like Elephant's, a coat like Sable's, and horns like Kudu's—Zebra trotted as fast as she could across the plain to the cave.

But once there, what disappointment was in store! There wasn't a single pair of horns left anywhere— only two odd ones that Rhino, in his shortsightedness, was at that moment claiming.

As for coats, there didn't seem to be any of those left, either.

And then Zebra saw it! The last coat, the worst coat—a loud and garish coat in vulgar black and white stripes, lying unwanted on the trampled earth.

"How they'll laugh and jeer at me if I go back in that," said Zebra. "And hornless."

Tears welled in her eyes. But suddenly something about the coat caught her attention. It was as if loud and garish wasn't so bad after all. As if loud and garish was even rather pleasing. Hurriedly, she picked up the coat, shook it out, and tried it on.

And immediately she knew she'd never take it off.

"It was made for me!" she cried. "A perfect fit! And anyway, who wants a dull coat like everyone else's and big, clumsy, complicated horns?"

Then, feeling very comfortable with herself, she trotted back across the plain to the lake.

When she arrived, however, the other animals couldn't stop laughing.

"Hello, Hornless!" they shouted and jeered. "Hello, Hornless, who was so busy eating she got the loud and garish coat no one else wanted!"

But Zebra didn't hear them. For Zebra didn't really care. By now she'd discovered what it was about the coat that had so pleased her. It was the HUGE mouth with its HUGE rubbery lip!

"Which couldn't be more perfect," she said, hungrily eyeing a huge clump of juicy, green grass, "for someone whose only thought is just another mouthful . . .

    and another

        and another

           and another

              and another . . ."

HOW THE HIPPO LOST HIS HAIR

Once long ago, Hippo had fur. A beautiful nut-brown coat of the thickest, silkiest fur ever seen. And how proud he was of it!

He strutted through the forest and along the riverbank, waving his beautiful silken tail and insisting that the other animals admire him.

"Am I not elegant? Is my coat not the thickest and silkiest you have ever seen?" he demanded.

Most of the other animals turned away at such boasting. But the monkeys in the trees fell all over themselves to agree.

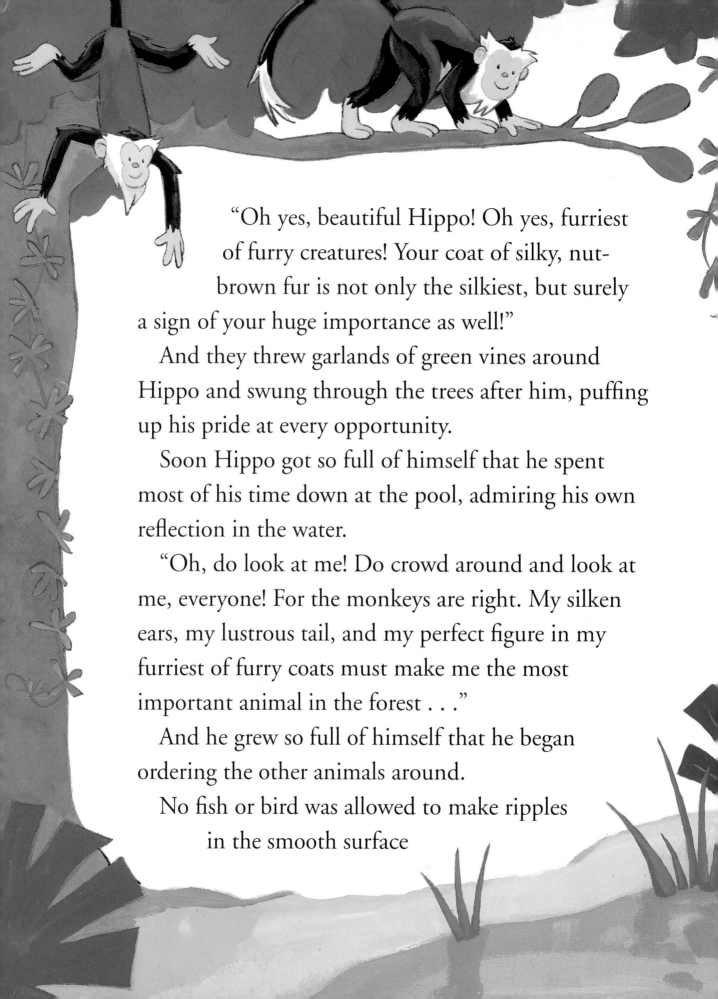

"Oh yes, beautiful Hippo! Oh yes, furriest of furry creatures! Your coat of silky, nut-brown fur is not only the silkiest, but surely a sign of your huge importance as well!"

And they threw garlands of green vines around Hippo and swung through the trees after him, puffing up his pride at every opportunity.

Soon Hippo got so full of himself that he spent most of his time down at the pool, admiring his own reflection in the water.

"Oh, do look at me! Do crowd around and look at me, everyone! For the monkeys are right. My silken ears, my lustrous tail, and my perfect figure in my furriest of furry coats must make me the most important animal in the forest . . ."

And he grew so full of himself that he began ordering the other animals around.

No fish or bird was allowed to make ripples in the smooth surface

of the pool while he was admiring his reflection. Birds had to groom him on command. Hare had to remove thorns from his feet on demand. As the furriest and most important animal in the forest, Hippo insisted on being first to feed on the juiciest plants in the forest and first to drink from the river after the rains.

And if any of the other animals disobeyed him, he threw terrible tantrums and made menacing threats. Finally, they could stand no more and called a meeting deep in the forest—far from Hippo's haunts.

"Hippo is out of control," one said.

"Our lives are no longer our own!" another added.

"Hippo must go! Hippo must go!" they chanted.

"No, wait," said Hare, stepping into their circle. "Surely it is not Hippo but Hippo's beautiful fur coat that is behind his impossible behavior."

"Well . . . yes . . . probably . . . you are right . . ." the other animals muttered.

"In that case," said Hare, "I have a plan. Follow my instructions exactly, and we will see what we will see."

So the animals followed Hare's instructions. First they collected as much dry grass as they could find and piled it up under the great Muula Tree on the edge of Hippo's sleeping spot.

Then, when Elephant lifted his trunk, smelled the air, and announced that a storm was brewing, they spread the grass in a thick circle around Hippo's sleeping spot.

And when Hippo demanded to know what they were up to, they said exactly what Hare had told them to say.

"O fairest of furry creatures, most noble and important Hippo, we are making your quarters snug and warm, for winter is coming, and we cannot have the cold wind ruffling such a beautiful fur coat as yours!"

Then, as the storm blackened
the skies and the thunder rumbled
in the distance and Hippo
snuggled down in his warm spot,
they ran to hide themselves on the
farthest side of the forest, exactly as
Hare had said they should. And as they ran off, Hare
crouched behind a clump of grass near the river to will
his plan to work and see what he would see.

One. Came the first bolt of lightning, sizzling
through the sky.

Two. Came the second bolt, lighting up the night.

"Come on, come on," whispered Hare. "Third
time's a charm! Come on!"

And three. Came the third-time's-a-charm bolt
of lightning, striking the great Muula Tree
and sending a snake of fire down through its
branches to the circle of dry grass around Hippo.

And within moments it was a wall of leaping, crackling flames. And Hippo was no longer snug or sleeping. He was careening from side to side in panic, until his long hair caught fire, too, and he had no choice but to charge out of his burning, sleeping quarters and—CHOWOWITZ!—plunge into the river.

Then Hare stood on the riverbank and stared at the dark, rippling waters. For a moment he thought he'd gone too far, and Hippo—not just his fur coat— was gone forever. But he needn't have worried. For as the rain began to fall like tears, Hare saw a pair of once-silken ears appear, followed by a pair of once-furry nostrils. With a huge sigh of relief, he set off for the far side of the forest to find the other animals.

"It worked!" he cried when he reached them. "How it worked! Hippo's safe, but the source of all his pride and his terrible behavior is gone. Our lives will be our own once more."

And Hare was right. When morning came and Hippo squelched out of the river and took a look at himself in the pool, he found he was now a great hairless creature with frizzled ears, no lustrous tail, and worst of all, no silken, nut-brown fur coat. He raced back to the river, and with an enormous MVUUUU, MVUUUU, he breathed all the air from his lungs and sank gratefully into it.

And it is there he has lived ever since, only coming up for air when he has to and only coming out to graze on the edge of the forest under cover of night. That's when the animals who knew him in his silken, nut-brown days are fast asleep.

TORTOISE LONGS TO FLY

Tortoise was lying in the sun when he overheard the other animals talking about him in the bushes.

"Tortoise is so slow and plain," he heard, "it's hard to keep a straight face watching him."

This upset Tortoise terribly. He felt his pride sting like soft skin pricked by sharp thorns. He thought of crawling into a dark cave and staying there for a long time. Then he had an idea and went to find Osprey.

"Good morning, Tortoise! How are you, my friend?" Osprey was so great and strong, he never felt the need to look down on others.

"Very well," Tortoise lied.

"And what can I do for you?" asked Osprey.

"You can come to dinner," said Tortoise.

"What a delightful idea," said Osprey. "I would love to."

So that evening Osprey joined Tortoise and his wife for dinner. And what a feast it was. Tortoise and his wife had outdone themselves.

"Why," said Osprey, "this is the best dinner I've ever eaten. And as for these bananas! Where do you get them?"

"Aha," said Tortoise. "That's a family secret! But since you have enjoyed everything so much, you must come again."

"I'd be honored," said Osprey, and he meant it.

And after that the great Osprey regularly went to dinner at Tortoise's. And as Tortoise had hoped, the other animals noticed and were most impressed.

"Well, he can't be all that slow and plain if the great and good Osprey spends so much time with him," they marveled.

And Tortoise heard them and started to feel cheerful about himself again. But not for long. Spiteful, sharp-tongued Chameleon made sure of that.

"So when will your great friend Osprey invite you to dinner in his nest?" he asked.

"Oh, he has," said Tortoise. "He asks me all the time. But so far I've been too busy to accept."

"Really?" said Chameleon cruelly. "Or are you just

unable to get there? Unless of course you are learning to fly!"

And once again, Tortoise felt as if he had been stuck with thorns.

"If only I could fly," he muttered angrily. "That would show them. And maybe, just maybe, I will!"

With a plan forming in his head, he went to find his wife and ask for her help.

First, as instructed, she invited Osprey to dinner. Next, with some difficulty, she carefully wrapped Tortoise in a bundle of banana leaves.

When Osprey arrived for dinner, she said, "Oh, Osprey, Tortoise had to make a sudden visit to see his sick mother. But by way of apology he asks you to accept this bunch of bananas—all wrapped up so they won't bruise on your way home."

And while Osprey was sorry about Tortoise's sick mother, he was very pleased about the bananas. He picked the bundle up in his beak and flew off to his nest, thinking of nothing but a big banana feast.

Tortoise, huddled inside the bundle, was thinking of nothing but how it would wipe the smile off the others' faces when they found he had flown to Osprey's for dinner!

But unfortunately, Tortoise's happy thoughts were quickly overcome by some very strange feelings: dizziness, panic, sickness, and fear.

"If this is what it feels like to fly," he thought, "then no wonder we leave it to the birds."

He bore it as long as he could—which wasn't long. "Hey, Osprey!" he soon yelled. "There's been a terrible mistake. Please, please, PUT ME DOWN!"

And Osprey, terrified at the idea of carrying a bunch of speaking bananas, opened his beak and gave a terrific squawk. And down went the bundle, Tortoise and all. KER-WHACKKK!

"Oh, my goodness!" Tortoise's wife cried when her husband eventually limped home. "What has Osprey done to you?"

"Dropped me!" Tortoise almost wept. "From a great height. Right on my shell. And I'm sure it's terribly cracked."

"Well," she answered. "Cracked it certainly is. All over. In a crisscross sort of way. But you know, I think Osprey may have done you a favor. It's a great improvement."

And that was the opinion of all.

"Very elegant, so interesting, very beautiful indeed!" the other animals raved.

Even Chameleon had to admit that in his new patterned shell, there was nothing plain about Tortoise.

And since Tortoise was the first tortoise, to this day there are those who insist that this is how the crisscross-patterned beauty of tortoise shells was born.

THE HOUSE THAT BUILT ITSELF

Once Wildcat and Hyena were neighbors.
They were bad neighbors.
They watched each other like hawks.

Neither could bear the other to have anything he or she didn't have.

So when Wildcat told Hyena she was going to look for a good place to build a new house, it was not surprising that Hyena said, "That's funny, Wildcat, I was going to do the same thing today."

Now, although Wildcat set off in one direction and Hyena set off in another, they were soon traveling along the same path—and Wildcat got ahead.

"Aha!" she said when she arrived at a perfect place. "If I build here, Hyena won't be able to, and I'll have a house in a beautiful spot and Hyena won't."

And immediately she started clearing the ground. When she got tired, she went off to rest in a shady tree. And while she was resting, Hyena arrived.

"Well, well!" he cried.

"What a good spot for a house this is. The ground has cleared itself. Now I can prepare the poles."

So Hyena cut down some trees, prepared the poles, and went off to eat lunch.

And while he was eating lunch, Wildcat returned.

"Oh my, oh my!" she cried. "What a very good spot this is. The poles have prepared themselves. Now I can put them up."

So Wildcat put up the poles. When she finished, the sun was setting, so she went to bed in a nearby thicket.

And while she was snoring, Hyena returned.

"Oh, what an excellent spot!" he cried. "Here the work does itself. First the ground clears itself, then the poles put themselves up. Now, by the light of the moon, I can cut the bamboo."

So Hyena cut the bamboo. When he finished, dawn was breaking, so he went off for an early breakfast.

35

And while he was breakfasting, Wildcat returned.

"Now this really is a perfect place!" she cried. "A place where the work does itself! First the poles prepare themselves, then the bamboo cuts itself. Now I can weave the bamboo."

So Wildcat wove the bamboo between the poles. When she was finished, the sun was high, so she went off for a long, cool drink.

And while she was drinking, Hyena returned.

"Ho ho!" he cried. "Better and better. First the ground clears itself, next the poles put themselves up, then the bamboo weaves itself. Now I can cut the grass for the thatch roof."

So Hyena cut the
thatching grass and
went off to see the
local sights.

And while he was
seeing the sights,
Wildcat returned.

"Ha ha!" she cried.
"What luck! What luck!
First the poles prepare
themselves, next the bamboo cuts itself, and then the
grass jumps off its stalks. Now all I have to do is
thatch the roof."

So Wildcat thatched the roof, admired her new
house from every angle, and set off for her old house
to move her
possessions.

And while she was gone, Hyena returned.

"Just as I'd hoped!" he cried. "The roof has thatched itself. The house is built! Now all I have to do is divide the house in two: one room for my wife—once I find one—and one room for me."

So Hyena divided the house, admired it from all sides, and set off for his old house to move his possessions.

And while he was gone, Wildcat returned and marveled that the house had divided itself.

"One room for me and one room for my husband once I get one!"

Then she moved in to one of the rooms.

And while she was unpacking, Hyena returned with his possessions and moved in to the other room.

But then, Hyena accidentally dropped a cooking pot—CRASH!—and Wildcat dropped a cooking pot—CLATTER!

And Hyena was so frightened by the clatter that he dropped another cooking pot—SMASH!

And Wildcat was so frightened by the smash that she dropped all her cooking pots—CRASH! SMASH! CLATTER! SHATTER!

And terrified that the house was haunted, they both dashed out the door, Hyena first, Wildcat second—and ran.

How they ran! They ran for days and kept on running until one day they ran into each other.

"Hello, Wildcat," said Hyena, "what's happened to you? Did you ever find a perfect spot to build that house?"

"Oh, I found a spot all right!" said Wildcat. "A beautiful spot, where most of the work did itself!"

"That's funny," said Hyena. "I, too, found a spot where most of the work did itself. The ground cleared itself, the poles put themselves up, the bamboo wove itself, and the roof thatched itself. But when the house was built and I moved in, something drove me out . . ."

"And when my house was built and I moved in," exclaimed Wildcat, "something drove *me* out . . ."

But here Wildcat stopped speaking and started running again. So did Hyena.

And to this day Wildcat and Hyena have never looked each other in the eye for fear of seeing their own foolishness reflected there.

And they've certainly never been neighbors!

COUNTING LEOPARD'S SPOTS

Leopard was admiring his spots in a pool one day, when suddenly Crocodile's head broke the surface and disturbed his reflection.

"Admiring your spots again, Leopard?"

"Wouldn't everyone if they had as many as I?" answered Leopard. "I mean, have you ever seen so many truly beautiful spots in one place?"

Crocodile heaved himself up onto the bank. "For my part, I cannot see the point of spots. Any spots at all. But," he said, heaving closer, "since you are longing to tell me, I'd like to know. How many do you have exactly?"

Leopard stepped back sharply.

Crocodile was far too close for comfort, and his question was extremely uncomfortable, too.

"Er, naturally I can't count my own spots. Nobody could. Nobody can. But, since you are so clever, perhaps you'd be good enough to count them for me—from over there, if you please."

But Crocodile, who could not count, only slipped slyly back into the water, snapping, "Crocodiles have better things to do than count spots."

Leopard waited for the surface of the pool to settle and took another look at himself.

"Drat that Croc," he muttered. "I was perfectly content with many spots. Now I'll never be happy until I know exactly how many spots. Drat. Drat. Drat."

He padded off up the bank and into the woods, dratting Crocodile under his breath until he met Warthog.

"Hello, Leopard," said Warthog. "Why are you dratting Crocodile under your breath?"

Immediately Leopard brightened.

"For no reason that you can't help with," he said. "If you'll just be a good sport and count my spots . . ."

"Very well," said Warthog, who could only count to five. "I don't mind. I'll count your spots. One, two, three, four, five. Um, yes, there you are, five. You most definitely have five spots."

"Definitely five!" Leopard was in seventh heaven. "Thank you, Warthog, thank you!"

And he padded off deeper into the woods, thanking Warthog under his breath until he met Elephant.

"Hello, Spotty," said Elephant, "and why are you thanking Warthog in that seventh-heaven, under-your-breath way?"

"Because he has told me how many spots I have," said Leopard. "And it's five."

Elephant, who could count, but only to ten (though he could also add ten to ten), nearly choked on a mouthful of thorn tree.

"Five spots! Is Warthog blind? Here, let me try."

Leopard arranged himself for easier counting.

Elephant took his time, chewing as he counted. "One, two, three, four, five, six, seven, eight, nine, ten." Then he counted another ten and added the two together. "There you are. There it is. Twenty spots. That's what you have. A definite twenty."

"A definite twenty?" cried Leopard.

"And that's a lot more than five," said Elephant.

"A lot more than five!" Leopard was seeing stars he was so excited. "Well, thank you a lot more than Wartie, Elephant. Thank you, thank you!"

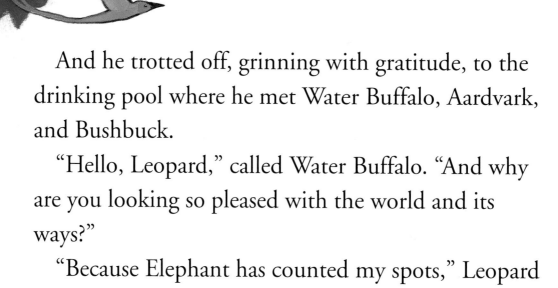

And he trotted off, grinning with gratitude, to the drinking pool where he met Water Buffalo, Aardvark, and Bushbuck.

"Hello, Leopard," called Water Buffalo. "And why are you looking so pleased with the world and its ways?"

"Because Elephant has counted my spots," Leopard said. "And do you know how many I have? Twenty!"

At this, Aardvark, who believed she could
count to fifty, nearly choked on a drink of water.

"Twenty spots! Is Elephant blind? Here, let me try.
I'll start with your tail."

So Leopard stretched out for easier counting, and
Aardvark began.

"One, two, three, four, five, six, seven, eight, nine,
ten, eleven, twelve, thirteen . . ."

"Wait," interrupted Bushbuck. "You'd already counted this one."

"I did not," said Aardvark.

"Yes, you did," said Water Buffalo.

"And you missed this one," said Bushbuck. "And you didn't count that one. You'll have to start over."

So Aardvark started again.

This time she got to twenty-nine without losing count. But then her problems began.

"Ummm . . . twenty-nine, twenty-nine, um, what's after twenty-nine . . . I know it, I know it, I do, I do."

"Forty?" suggested Water Buffalo.

"No, no, twenty-eight, twenty-nine . . . thirty . . . that's it . . . thirty, thirty-six, thirty . . . no wait . . . this one was twenty-nine and this one was thirty, so I've counted these twice and I've missed this, so this is thirty-six, except I forgot thirty-one and thirty-two, didn't I? Oh dear . . ." Aardvark scratched her head. "Now I've completely lost count . . ."

"Lost count of what?" Tortoise asked curiously as he ambled up, craning his neck to see.

"My spots," said Leopard, leaping to his feet and shaking himself impatiently. "The truth is, Tortoise, now that that cruel Crocodile has brought the subject up, I'll never be content until I know how many beautiful spots I have."

At this, Tortoise blinked kindly.

"In that case, dear Leopard, allow me . . ."

And slowly and deliberately, Tortoise began.

"Light, dark, light, dark, light, dark," he counted until he'd pointed out every spot on Leopard's coat.

"So there it is," he announced. "You have two spots, Leopard. Light spots and dark spots. Know it and be happy."

And a little later, Leopard returned to the pool to take a new look at himself and to tell his handsome reflection what he now knew:

"The number of spots on your beautiful coat depends on who's counting."

LAZY LION, QUICK-THINKING HARE

ion was lazing in the sun one day when he saw Hare hurrying, scurrying, and bustling. It gave him an idea.

"Hare," he called, stretching and yawning. "Come and work for me and I'll give you three good meals a day, every day, and as much as you can eat."

For a moment Hare slowed down.

"And protection from Fox?" he bargained.

"And protection from Fox," agreed Lion.

"And protection from Jackal?" said Hare.

"And protection from Jackal," said Lion.

"Done," said Hare. "Then I am your servant."

"Good," said Lion. "Then prepare my supper and make my bed quickly."

Hurrying off, Hare immediately began to regret the agreement.

How could he be Lion's servant? He had enough to do just looking after himself. And besides, what did Lion eat? How did Lion like his bed made up?

He rushed around, this way and that, in and out, up and down, panicking but trying his best, until at last he'd prepared supper and made Lion's bed.

But when Lion stretched and yawned and strolled over to sit down for his supper, Hare was in for a shock.

"And what on the Great One's earth is this?" Lion roared. "You call this food? Why, it's nothing but a pile of leaves!"

"Er, yes, but pretty leaves, sir," stammered Hare. "And beautifully laid out for your pleasure, sir."

"Nonsense!" Lion roared. "Lions don't eat leaves. Pretty or otherwise. And since you have prepared nothing else and I am starving, I'm going to eat YOU!"

And he pounced.

But Hare was too quick for Lion, or so he thought.

He hopped down a hole between the roots of a tree—except for one leg.

And Lion caught it.

"Gotcha!" he roared.

But Hare was thinking quickly while holding onto a root inside the hole. He shouted, "Not so, sir. That's a root you're pulling at, sir, not me!"

And not wanting to look like a fool in front of his servant, Lion immediately let go of Hare's leg, which now appeared to be a root, and grabbed what he hoped might be Hare's leg, which actually was a root.

And Hare was free, though not for long.

The next morning, when Hare crept out of the hole, Lion was waiting for him.

"WHETHER I EAT YOU OR WHETHER I DON'T, YOU'RE STILL MY SERVANT. SO WHERE'S MY BREAKFAST, YOU LAZY—"

"Lazy?" Hare was deeply insulted. "Are you sure you're not talking about yourself, sir?"

"SILENCE!" roared Lion. "YOU KNOW WHAT HAPPENS TO SERVANTS WHO TALK BACK TO THEIR MASTERS? THIS . . ."

And once again, Lion pounced.

And once again, Hare was too quick for him, or so he thought.

He bounded away and would have made it except
that at the last minute his escape was blocked by a
deep and fast-flowing river.

There was no way across, and while Hare was
desperately searching for one, Lion caught up with
him and pounced.

And this time, Hare didn't get away.

But it didn't stop him from thinking quickly.

"Oh, sir, oh, master!" he cried from Lion's mouth. "Do whatever you like with me. Have me for breakfast, lunch, or supper. But please, please, PLEASE don't throw me across the river into the territory of my GREATEST enemy, the Hiriwashaboos. Anything, O lord and master, ANYTHING but that!"

"Aha!" Lion was delighted. "Now I know what I can do to teach this too-smart-for-his-own-good servant a lesson . . ."

And he took Hare from his mouth and hurled him with all his might across the water.

But Hare was ready.

He tucked his feet up tight, let the force of Lion's throw take him, and landed gracefully on the other side.

There he picked himself up and laughed at Lion. "Thank you, sir, thank you!" he said, hurrying off to enjoy his freedom.

But not for long.

Furious at being outwitted a second time, Lion rolled a fallen tree trunk into the river, jumped onto it, and paddled over to the other side.

"If it's the last thing I do," he snarled as he clambered up the bank, "I'll get that Hare."

He hunted high.

He hunted low.

He hunted by day. He hunted by night.

But when the sun got too hot, he took shelter in a cool cave.

And there in the cave, fast asleep, he found Hare.

"Gotcha!" roared Lion.

And pounced.

But even from asleep to awake, Hare was too fast for him—and too quick-thinking.

In one bound he was on his feet at the mouth of the cave, standing under an overhanging rock and pretending to hold it up.

"Oh, master, oh, sir!" he cried. "This is no place to take shelter. Can't you see? The roof of this cave is falling in. Quick! Help me hold it up or we will both be crushed to dust!"

And, horrified at the thought, Lion bounded over, placed his huge paws under the great rock, and began pushing upward with all his might.

After a while Hare, who was still pretending to push beside him, said, "Sir, you must be getting mighty tired, sir. Let me go and collect some rocks to build a pillar that will hold up the roof in your place. Only whatever you do, don't let go until I get back, or you'll certainly be done for . . ."

"All right," grunted Lion. "But hurry!"

So Hare hurried off.

In fact, he hopped, skipped, and jumped off, leaving Lion to hold up the roof—not forever, but long enough . . .

Long enough for Lion to realize he'd been outwitted once more—and that took long enough!

The Tortoises' hard work in their garden had paid off: they had ripe pumpkins, pineapples, and lots of sweet potatoes.

But Tortoise's wife wasn't satisfied. "Oh, for a change of diet," she sighed. "Oh, for a bag of corn."

"If it's corn you want, my dear," Tortoise said generously, "then corn is what you shall have. I'll take some of our produce to market and exchange it for a bag of corn."

So though it was hot outside, Tortoise placed two pumpkins, two pineapples, and lots of sweet potatoes in a basket, balanced it on his back, and set off. He loved his wife very much.

The basket was heavy. The way was long. The sun was boiling hot. Suddenly, Tortoise heard the inviting babble of a stream. He couldn't resist. He put the basket down on the beaten path and clambered through the undergrowth for a long, cool drink.

But while he was happily refreshing himself, who should come down the path but Monkey.

"Goodness gracious!" she cried, seeing the basket lying unattended. "It must be my birthday!" And with a very naughty chuckle she picked it up, placed it over her arm, and sauntered off into the shade to have a feast.

When Tortoise returned from the stream and realized the basket was missing, he was beside himself. "It can't be!" he cried. "It was right here and now it's not. No one would be so mean as to take it."

"Wouldn't they?" asked Butterfly, who had witnessed the whole scene. "Then take a look over there in the shade."

Tortoise looked and could hardly believe what he saw.

Greedily and wastefully, Monkey had taken bites out of several potatoes and was already halfway through a pumpkin.

"Stop that at once!" Tortoise shouted. "That basket and all that is in it is mine!"

"Sorry," Monkey grinned, "but I don't know what you're talking about. I found this basket lying unattended on the path."

"That's because I put it there while I had a drink from the stream!" Tortoise yelled. "And if you won't

give it back to me this minute, I'll take my case to Elephant."

"Then do that," said Monkey, cheerfully spitting pumpkinseeds. "Because I know the law around here even if you don't, and it's finders keepers on the beaten path."

But Tortoise was not so hot under the shell that he wasn't listening.

Elephant knew jungle law, and he was holding court that evening. Determined to get justice, Tortoise presented his case. Butterfly supported it. So did Lizard, who had also seen the whole thing.

But Monkey was unrepentant. "There is no case," she said, swinging in with the basket on her arm and a whole troop of relatives to support her. "The basket was lying unattended on the beaten path. I found it. I keep it. Tell me that isn't the law."

Elephant shuffled and muttered into his trunk. "Unfortunately," he trumpeted softly, "Monkey is right. Finders keepers *is* the law in these parts. As much as it pains me, Tortoise—for I know how much work you and your wife put into the garden—Monkey keeps the basket and all that's in it."

Monkey and her relatives screeched with delight and scampered off, leaving Tortoise deeply upset at what he felt was a terrible injustice.

However, it was not Tortoise's nature to stay low for long.

"I tell you what, my dear," he said to his wife. "I'll go and visit my brother and see if he can spare a few cobs of corn to cheer us up."

And so the next morning Tortoise set out along the path that led to his brother's. As always, the way was long and the sun was hot. He was just thinking about taking a short rest, when he saw something ahead in the path that made his heart miss a beat.

Surely it isn't, he reasoned with himself. Surely it can't be . . .

But he crept closer and saw that it was. Monkey— no doubt stuffed with sweet potatoes, pumpkin, and pineapple—was fast asleep on the side of the path.

Her tail, however, lay on the path.

The sight made Tortoise dizzy with excitement.

"I'll show you the law!" he cried. "And how to uphold it!" And without further ado, he clamped Monkey's tail hard in his mouth and began to move off.

"Hey! Stop! Stop thief! What are you doing with my tail?" Monkey screeched.

Luckily for Tortoise, who couldn't open his mouth to answer, at that moment Butterfly fluttered by. "Looks to me, Monkey, as if Tortoise found your tail

lying on the path and is keeping it," she laughed.

"Looks like that to me, too." Even luckier for Tortoise, Elephant happened to be nearby and emerged from a thicket. "Of course," he trumpeted, "you are welcome to bring your case to court, Monkey. But I can tell you now you'll be wasting your time, for in this case, as in the basket case, finders will be keepers. So go ahead, Tortoise, bite it off and take it home to your wife for a fly whisk."

"Nooooo! No! Please!" Monkey screeched. "Not my precious tail. Not a fly whisk. Anything but that. Look, listen, give me back my tail and I'll give you back your basket and a bag of sweet potatoes!"

"Not enough," Elephant trumpeted. "Not for saving a tail from becoming a fly whisk. The basket, a bag of sweet potatoes, and a bag of corn! By tomorrow afternoon."

Then very sulkily, Monkey agreed—what choice did she have?

And, smiling to himself, Tortoise let go of her tail, thanked Elephant profoundly, and made his way home.

And though supper that night was still pumpkin and sweet potatoes, he and his wife ate it with the greatest relish, knowing that justice had found its own way of being done.

RABBIT'S ROPE TRICK

Elephant was busy tearing and ripping and uprooting trees.

He was so busy with the tearing and ripping and munching and uprooting that he almost stepped on Rabbit.

"Excuse me," said Rabbit, barely springing out of the way in time. "Why don't you look where you're trampling?"

"Sorry," mumbled Elephant through a mouthful of crunchy leaves, "but you are really so small and insignificant, you can't expect a great creature such as myself to notice you."

Rabbit felt deeply insulted.

She felt hot and bothered.

She felt furious.

"Size isn't everything!" she shouted, hopping up and down. "I'm smart. Very smart. And there's strength in brains, you know!"

"Really?" said Elephant, nearly stepping on her again. "Can't say that I've noticed."

"All right," Rabbit cried. "Then I'll make you notice. I challenge you to a game of tug-of-war!"

For a moment Elephant stopped munching and looked down at Rabbit with his mouth open.

"That's nonsense. You know I'd beat you in a game of tug-of-war. I'd beat any animal in a game of tug-of-war."

"Fine," said Rabbit. "You wait here, and I'll get the rope. And we will see."

And then, since Rabbit was smart and did have brains, she wasted no time.

She scampered down to the river, stopped at the bank, and pretended to roll around laughing.

And when Hippo surfaced to ask what was so funny, she only laughed harder.

"Oh, what a silly old thing you are," she said. "I'm laughing because you think you're so strong, but even I could beat you in a game of tug-of-war."

"I'd like to see you try!" Hippo snorted indignantly. "Why, you're so small and feeble, I'd say you have less strength in your whole body than I have in a few hairs in my ear."

"Fine," said Rabbit, "you wait here. I'll get the rope. And we will see."

Then she raced off into the forest. She gathered some long, strong pieces

of vine, plaited them together to make a long, strong rope, and returned to the riverbank.

"Here you are, Hippo!" she called. "Here's your end of the rope."

Hippo waded out of the water in disbelief. "Really, this is ridiculous . . ." he began. "It's undignified for me to have a game of tug-of-war with a rabbit."

But Rabbit was already tying the rope around one of Hippo's legs.

"Now," she said, "since the rope is so long, you might not see me on the other end, but I'll be there,

and when you hear me shout PULL, start pulling."

Then, picking up the other end of the rope, she
scampered back to the trees to Elephant.

"Here you are, Elephant. This is your end of the
rope. Since it's a rather long rope, you probably
won't see me on the other end, but I'll be there.
When you hear me shout PULL, start pulling!"
And while Elephant reluctantly picked up the
rope and wound it around his trunk a few times,
Rabbit ran off to hide in a clump of grass exactly
halfway between Elephant in the trees and Hippo on
the riverbank.

"Are you ready?" she shouted at the top of her voice. "Are you steady? For the great tug-of-war? PULL!"

And Elephant and Hippo pulled.

They pulled, they tugged, they dug in their heels, and they yanked. They braced themselves hard and braced themselves harder.

They pulled and tugged and yanked their hardest.

Hardly able to control her laughter, Rabbit lay in the grass and listened to their struggle.

And only when she decided she'd taught them both a good lesson did she yell at the top of her voice, "IT'S A DRAW! THE TUG-OF-WAR GAME IS DECLARED A DRAW!"

Then, rubbing herself down with dirt so it looked as if she'd been engaged in a struggle, Rabbit sauntered over to Elephant.

"Small and insignificant, with no strength?" she said. "Is that how you'd describe me now?"

"Certainly not," panted Elephant. "From now on, it's little but mighty."

"As small and feeble as the hairs in your ear?" Rabbit said, strolling over to Hippo. "Is that how you'd describe me now?"

"Oh no, not at all," panted Hippo. "Now I'd say Rabbit may be small, but she's strength itself."

And that evening, when the animals gathered for a drink at the water hole to talk about Rabbit's triumph, it was not surprising that neither Elephant nor Hippo dared show their faces.

Which for Rabbit was just as well. For if they had, they would have soon realized how they'd been tricked. And if Elephant hadn't hurled her to the crows, Hippo probably would have thrown her to the crocs.

BUSHBUCK AND THE CRAFTY CHAMELEON

Bushbuck and Chameleon were quarreling. Toad was siding with Bushbuck.

"But my message for Lemur was urgent," said Bushbuck. "And you took two days to deliver it."

"Yes," said Toad. "You criticize Tortoise for being slow, yet you are the slowest of all."

"I am not slow. I'm not, I'm not!" Chameleon declared, his tongue darting. "I can be fast. I can be as fast as you, Bushbuck, if I care to be."

At this Bushbuck and Toad laughed heartily, for everyone knew that Bushbuck was one of the fastest animals.

"I tell you what," chuckled Toad, "why don't the two of you have a race. Then, Chameleon, if you win, the rest of us will have to admit you're not slow."

"What an interesting idea," said Chameleon, rolling his eyes. "How about first thing tomorrow morning. We could start here at our watering hole and finish at Lion's Rock."

Then he disappeared—or rather blended—into his favorite tree to eat mosquitoes and plan how he, slow-moving Chameleon, might beat fast and fleet Bushbuck in a race.

"There must be a way," he said to each terrified mosquito on the end of his tongue. "Tell me how I can beat Bushbuck in a race and I'll let you go."

"Cheat!" the mosquitoes whined feebly.

"Of course I'll cheat!" Chameleon snapped, swallowing them anyway. "The question is how to go about it."

And then, in a flash that made him blush bright red all over, the answer stared him in the face.

"I'll cheat the way I always cheat," he grinned. "I'll be where I'm not expected to be. And how I shall enjoy it. Not only the winning but every minute of the race, too."

So, rising before dawn the next morning, Chameleon made his way down to the watering hole.

There he collected some berries—the berries all the animals knew not to eat because they made them terribly thirsty. He carefully smeared them on a clump of fresh green grass before climbing into a nearby tree to wait for Bushbuck.

And as soon as the sun rose, Bushbuck galloped over.

"Good morning," said Chameleon brightly.

"Where are you?" said Bushbuck. "Right above you, ready to start. But perhaps you should have some breakfast first. That clump of grass there looks utterly scrum-dumptious."

"It certainly does," said Bushbuck, beginning to munch at the grass. When he had finished, he licked his lips thirstily and looked up into the tree.

"Still there, Chameleon? Still ready?"

"Oh yes," said Chameleon.

"Good," said Bushbuck. "Then I'll just take a drink and we can begin."

With great satisfaction, Chameleon watched Bushbuck drinking thirstily.

The first part of my crafty plan is working, he thought, his tongue darting with excitement. Now for the second part.

"Okay!" he called down when Bushbuck finally finished drinking. "We must decide on our starting signal. What if I call 'Ready! Set! Go!' and drop a twig onto your head. That will be the signal to begin the race."

"Fine by me," said Bushbuck.

"All right," said Chameleon, taking a deep breath and bracing himself. "Ready! Set! Go!"

And with that, Chameleon let himself—not a twig—fall out of the tree and onto Bushbuck's head.

And thinking he felt the starting signal, Bushbuck took off.

Effortlessly and easily, he sped through the bush like an arrow, quite unaware that clinging lightly to one of his horns, eyes bulging with pleasure, was his opponent in the race—the crafty Chameleon.

In fact, so unaware of Chameleon's presence and so certain of winning was he, that Bushbuck decided to stop at a stream along the way and try to quench his terrible thirst.

Then, as he raced toward Lion's Rock and the finish line, he stopped again.

"Why, that poor, slow Chameleon will hardly have left the starting post," he chuckled as he bent his head gracefully to the water.

But when Bushbuck raised his head and looked toward Lion's Rock, he couldn't believe his eyes.

A loud burst of applause and cheering erupted from the crowd of animals waiting at the finish line.

"Amazing! What an upset! Chameleon's the winner in the great Bushbuck-Chameleon race!" someone cried.

With a few bounds Bushbuck was at the rock and staring in disbelief.

Somehow, impossibly, Chameleon was already there.

"But you can't be . . ." Bushbuck stammered.

"Well, I am," Chameleon grinned. "For all to see. And now I want a proper public apology from you and Toad for calling me slow."

Bushbuck groaned inwardly. The last thing he felt like doing was apologizing to Chameleon, whom he didn't trust more than he could see him, which usually wasn't at all.

"Er . . . um," he muttered.

But before he needed to go further, Lemur made an unexpected entrance from the trees.

"Hi, everyone. Hi! What's all the excitement about? And how on earth did you get Bushbuck to let you ride on one of his horns like that, Chameleon?"

A hush fell over the crowd.

Toad finally broke the silence. "Lemur, what do you mean?"

"Oh, I was swinging around in the trees," said Lemur innocently, "when I looked down and saw Bushbuck racing along with a lump on one of his horns. When he stopped for a drink at the Lion's Rock

watering hole, I realized the lump wasn't a lump at all but Chameleon climbing onto an overhanging branch, changing colors, and making his way over here."

The animals turned at once on Chameleon.

"You cheater!" they cried. "You crafty, conniving trickster!"

But their yelling didn't last long.

For although Chameleon was there all right, no one could see him, and shouting at nothing soon made them all feel ridiculous.

As for Chameleon, he had no regrets.

Being called a crafty, conniving trickster was almost a compliment, especially when he considered what his craftiness had won him—the incredible sensation, the incomparable, wind-whistling feeling of racing at a high speed.

And besides, from his invisible position he could now see Bushbuck returning to the pool and drinking and drinking and drinking . . .

It's just as well for Chameleon that none of the others could see his crooked, crafty, satisfied smile.

JACKAL AND THE TALKING TREE

It had been a long, hot, rainless summer. There was little to drink and little to eat, and the animals were all very hungry.

Jackal sat in the shade of a tree, rubbing her tummy and groaning.

"Gimme food. Gimme food. Gimme something to eat. Gimme anything," she groaned.

Immediately, as if in answer to her prayer, there was a plop, and a slightly squashed, squishy-looking fruit landed on the ground beside her.

Jackal looked around nervously. Was someone playing a trick? She glanced up and saw that the tree

she was sitting under was laden with fruit. Why had she never noticed it before?

She got up and walked around the piece of fruit. She sniffed it carefully. She gave it a lick. She pushed it around with her paw for a while, then couldn't resist and gobbled it up.

"Delicious!" she sighed. "Now all I have to do is wait and see if it's poison."

When she didn't develop a pain in her tummy and two more of the fruits plopped down beside her, she gobbled those up, licked her lips, and set off to find her friend Rabbit and share her discovery.

But on the way she met Kudu. And since Kudu looked so hungry, Jackal couldn't resist telling him about the tree.

And on his way to the tree Kudu met Elephant and told him about it. And on his way to the tree Elephant met Eland and told him. And on his way to the tree Eland met Rhinoceros and told her.

On her way Rhinoceros met Gnu and told her. And on her way Gnu met Giraffe and told him, who told Hartebeest, who told Hare, who told Tortoise.

So when Jackal finally returned with Rabbit, they couldn't get anywhere near the tree or its fruit. It was surrounded by feeding animals.

"Oh dear," wailed Jackal. "I wish I'd kept this whole thing to myself. I suppose we'll have to leave for now and creep down here at sunrise to feed before anyone else is up."

But during the night news of the tree and its delicious fruit spread like wildfire.

When Jackal and Rabbit arrived early next morning, there was an even bigger crowd around the tree than the day before.

"And to think that I found it and I'm the one still starving!" complained Jackal. "We shall have to do something about this!"

And they did. The next morning, when Jackal and Rabbit arrived at the tree and found it surrounded by feeding animals, they did not complain.

Rabbit climbed onto a nearby anthill and made an announcement.

"Attention! Attention! Animals, stop stuffing yourselves and listen to me!"

And when they had all stopped to listen, she continued. "Surely, before we freely feed on the fruit of this tree, we had better find out whose tree it is."

The animals shuffled around uncomfortably. They knew that Rabbit was right, and that in their hunger they had behaved greedily and thoughtlessly.

"Very well," Kudu broke the silence. "We shall do the correct thing. But who shall we ask?"

"The tree, of course," said Rabbit. "Who else?"

Then Kudu pawed the ground, thrust back his horns, and called, "Tree? Tree? Can you hear me? Who do you belong to?" And when no answer came, Elephant flapped his ears. "Kudu is not addressing the tree properly. Here, let me try."

So Elephant lifted his trunk and trumpeted, "Tree! Mighty Tree! Generous Tree! Can you hear me? Please, in all your greatness, tell us who you are, on whose land you stand, and who you belong to!"

And from the topmost branches came the answer, loud and clear.

"My name is Muula, and the land I stand on is Jackal's land. Therefore I and all my fruits belong to Jackal, and none but Jackal shall eat them."

Then the animals bowed their heads in shame and

slowly wandered away. And when the last were out of sight, Jackal and Rabbit burst into fits of laughter as out of the top of the tree flew Osprey.

"Oh my, oh my, oh my," laughed Jackal. "Osprey, old friend, thank you, thank you. You played your part to perfection. Now come, let's celebrate and feast to our heart's content."

But that, though it could be, isn't the end of the story.

"This is repulsive!" cried Osprey at his first taste of the squishy fruit. "I'm hungry, but not that hungry!"

"Utterly disgusting!" agreed Rabbit. "So, my dear

Jackal, as Osprey and I don't like it and none of the other animals will dare touch it now, it would seem that the fruit of the Muula Tree is . . ."

"All mine!" said Jackal, munching happily.

And, true to say, it has been ever since.